SKA

NORTH
AMERICA

CALIFORNIA

QUÉBEC

CHICAGO    •BOSTON

A T L A N T I C

LONDON
EUROPE

LOUISIANA
FLORIDA

YUCATAN

GUATEMALA        JAMAICA

HONDURAS

O C E A N

AFRICA

F I C

I

C

A

N

PERU

SOUTH
AMERICA

3:00 4:00 5:00 6:00 7:00 8:00 9:00 10:00 11:00 12:00 1:00 2:00

LONDON        YUCATÁN        QUEBEC

# SOMEWHERE IN THE WORLD RIGHT NOW

*by Stacey Schuett*

Alfred A. Knopf • New York

*To Mavis and Frances,*
*for seeing beyond the horizon*

THIS IS A BORZOI BOOK PUBLISHED BY ALFRED A. KNOPF, INC.

Maps from *Goode's World Atlas* copyright © 1994 by Rand McNally, R.L. 91-S-244.
Used by permission of Rand McNally & Company

Library of Congress Cataloging-in-Publication Data

Schuett, Stacey.
Somewhere in the world right now / written and illustrated by Stacey Schuett.
p.   cm.
Summary: Describes what is happening in different places around the
world at a particular time.
ISBN 0-679-86537-3 (trade hardcover)—ISBN 0-679-96537-8 (lib. bdg.)
[1. Time—Fiction. 2. Geography—Fiction.] I. Title.
PZ7.S3855So   1994
[E]—dc20   94-6223

Manufactured in the United States of America
10 9 8 7 6 5 4 3 2 1

# A Note to the Reader

The earth is constantly turning on its axis. One full rotation takes 24 hours, and during that time, the position of the sun in the sky changes, creating light and dark, day and night.

It used to be that many places measured time from when the sun was highest overhead, at noon. But this meant that neighboring cities would have different clock times at the same instant. Faster travel and better communications made this inconvenient, so in 1884 an international agreement was reached to adopt a system of standard times. The planet was divided into 24 equal areas called time zones. (However, as the maps on the endpapers show, the time zones were adjusted to conform to geographical and political boundaries.) Everywhere within each zone, it is always the same time. When moving from one time zone to the next, there is a change in one hour, forward or backward, depending on whether one is moving east or west.

An important feature of the time zone system is the international date line. As the sun crosses the 24 time zones, somewhere a change in date must occur. The international community needed to agree on a boundary where the new date would begin. It's clear that to have the date change in the middle of a crowded country would cause much confusion, so the line was drawn through the Pacific Ocean, with a few jogs around inhabited regions. Since the earth turns eastward, places west of the date line move into the new date first. So, no matter where in the world you are, there's somewhere else where it's a different day!

*S*omewhere in the world right now, it's deepest night. Fog hugs the shoulders of buildings and bridges. A baker slides long loaves of bread into an oven. Somewhere, somebody watches a movie. A mouse hunts for crumbs.

Somewhere else, in velvety darkness,
elephants sleep standing up, swaying
gently from side to side.

Whales breach and dive in the sea, singing their low,
sweet songs. Penguins press close to their chicks to
keep them warm.

Somewhere, the night wind sighs and murmurs.
The moon shines through a window. A little girl
lies dreaming of tomorrow.

But somewhere else, right now, tomorrow is already here. Dawn is breaking. A rooster crows and people are waking up.

Somewhere, it's morning. Families eat breakfast. Kids get dressed for school. Farmers leave for the fields to tend their crops.

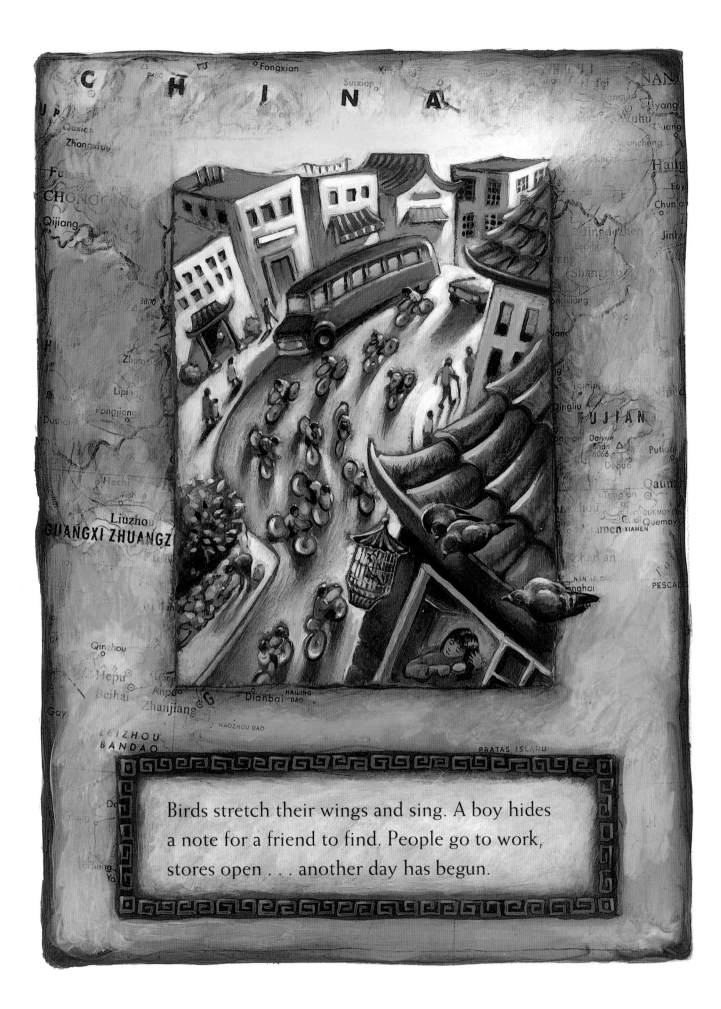

Birds stretch their wings and sing. A boy hides a note for a friend to find. People go to work, stores open . . . another day has begun.

And somewhere, right now, people buy food for their midday meal. A carpenter measures wood. A dog runs off with his lunch.

In the late morning shade, a baby kangaroo naps. A koala munches eucalyptus leaves.

Somewhere in the world right now, fishing boats return with their catch. Sea gulls swoop and dive and bicker over scraps.

Somewhere, the afternoon sun gilds workers in the vineyards. Cows graze and rest in the grass. A girl tends her horses.

Somewhere in the world right now, the sun
is setting. Monkeys screech from the trees
as a jaguar glides through the jungle. Parrots
mutter and chuckle. Shadows grow long.

North Chicago
Lake Forest
Highland Park
Winnetka
Wilmette
Evanston
CHICAGO
E.
Chicago

O I S

And somewhere else, the sun has already slipped
away, drawing evening down like a shade. In the
city, signs flash on and off, off and on. Trains
whoosh through tunnels, taking people home.

Watseka

Pawler

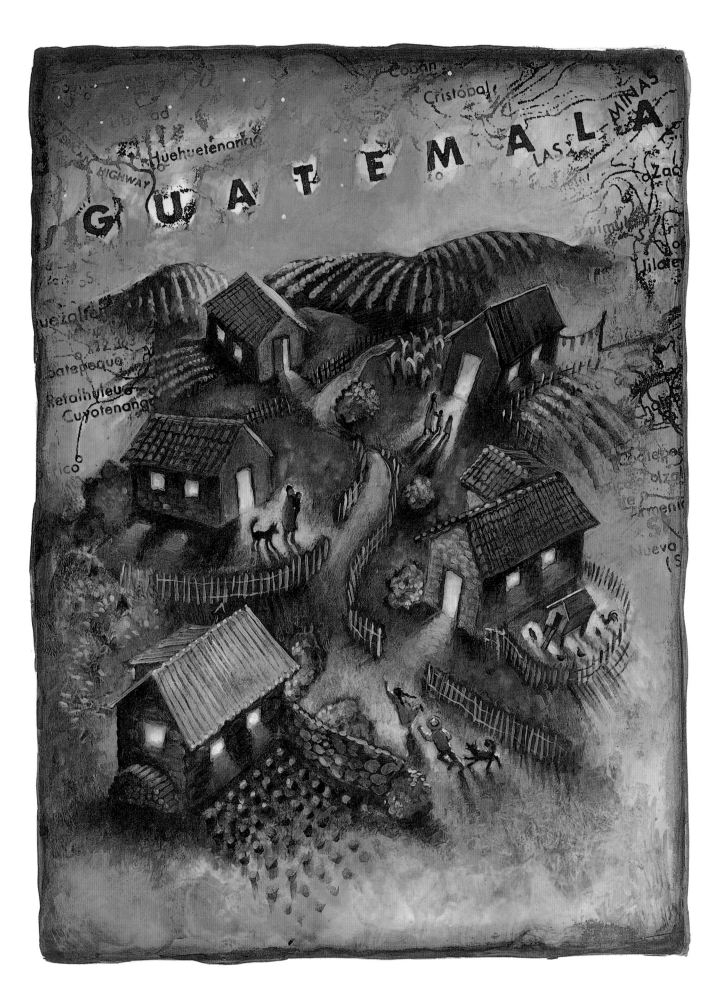

Somewhere, suddenly, houses light up. A girl and her brother race each other to the door.

The day's work is done. A family sits down to supper.

And somewhere else, night has fallen. Clouds
cushion the moon as it climbs across the sky.
An alligator sleeps in an inky swamp beneath
a tapestry of stars.

The last notes of a song fade into the rhythm of the waves.

Somewhere, a truck driver follows her headlights
down a lonely road. A night watchman starts his shift.

Friends say good night.

Somewhere, somebody reads a story, and someone listens.

Brookline

Voices whisper, "Sweet dreams," and under a blanket of night, lights go out one by one, somewhere in the world . . .

right now.